Lily
to the
Rescue

W. Bruce Cameron

Illustrations by
Richard Cowdrey

Scholastic, Inc.

LILY TO THE RESCUE

Copyright © 2018 by W. Bruce Cameron

Illustrations © 2018 by Richard Cowdrey

A Starscape Book
Published by Tom Doherty Associates
175 Fifth Avenue
New York, NY 10010

www.tor-forge.com

ISBN 978-1-338-36031-8

10 9 8 7 6 5 4 3 2 1   19 20 21 22 23

Printed in the U.S.A.   131
First printing 2019

Chapter 1

I had a mother and no sisters and too many brothers.

We all lived inside a clean, warm kennel. Our kennel had three walls that I couldn't see through and one that I could. The one I could see through was made of thin pieces of wire twisted together. I could glimpse what was on the other side, but I couldn't squeeze through. None of us could.

What I saw through the wire was another kennel just like ours, but empty. I could smell and hear other animals outside our kennels—there were dogs who barked and dogs who didn't and strange-smelling animals who were not dogs and made mewing sounds. Other not-dogs chattered or hissed. But I never saw any of these animals, and they didn't come into the kennel with us.

We had not always lived here. I remembered a different place with different smells. There, I was cold. In the kennel, I was not.

When we lived in the cold place, my meals were milk from my mother. In the kennel, I ate different food. The wall that I could see through opened up now and then, and a woman came in with soft mush in a bowl. My mother would greet this woman and lick her hands while her tail wagged happily, so I knew the lady was nice. She was safe. I could trust her.

I also liked her food very much. But I didn't always get to eat as much as I wanted.

That was because I had too many brothers.

The largest one was white with gray splotches, like me. Another was black with a white tip to his tail, and the third was brown all over. They all had soft ears and big paws and busy tails. So did I. But they were all bigger than I was. A lot bigger, which seemed to lead them to believe they could push me around.

It had always been hard for me to find a place to drink milk from my mother, because a brother or two would shoulder me aside. In the kennel, it was hard for me to gobble up enough meaty mush from the bowl, because my brothers wanted to get there first, and I couldn't always push my way in.

My brothers stepped on my face when we played. They slept on top of me until I felt flat. They were louder and quicker and rougher than I was, and when we played, I always ended up on the bottom of the pile.

Sometimes I thought life would be easier without brothers.

If a brother bit my tail or fell down on my head or stuck a paw in my eye, I yipped or squealed. Then my mother would come to find me. She'd pick me up by the back of my neck and carry me to a corner of our kennel where there was a scrap of carpet on the floor. There she'd lie down with me. Her body curled into a circle with me at the center. Sometimes, when my brothers were being too rough and I was whimpering, I could feel the gentle bite of my mother's teeth on the nape of my neck before her mouth was even there, feel her warm breath, all in my imagination.

I loved lying with my mother. She was a girl dog, just like me. I could smell it. We were the only two girls in our kennel. I thought that was why she loved me best.

Sometimes when I was curled up with my mother, I watched people walk by our kennel. They didn't usually stop unless they were bringing us food.

But one day they did stop. I picked up my head with interest.

The woman who brought us food was there, but there were other people, too. Smaller people who moved more quickly and a bit more clumsily than she did.

Young humans. Children.

My nose twitched. I could smell two boys and a girl. The boys were bigger; the girl was smaller. This was familiar—just like *my* family!

My brothers were piled up in a heap by a wall of the kennel. Brown-Brother was chewing on a toy. Biggest-Brother was chewing on Brown-Brother's leg. White-Tail-Brother was about to jump on Biggest-Brother's head.

"Oh!" said the girl on the other side of the wire. It was a long, drawn-out sound that had both happiness and longing in it. "Oh, puppies!"

I got up and shook myself and trotted forward to investigate.

The girl knelt down and stuck her fingers through the wire. I sniffed at them. They smelled wonderful. I could smell salty sweat and soft skin and dirt and something sticky and sweet. She giggled when I started licking.

Then all three of my brothers barreled into me.

Before I knew it, I was buried under wagging, panting, yipping brothers.

"Get out of the way, Maggie Rose!" I heard someone say.

I wiggled, backing up. When I pulled my head out of the pile of brothers, I saw that the girl was no longer kneeling by the wire. Her brothers had pushed her to one side so that they could kneel down and put their own fingers into our kennel and laugh as my brothers licked and nibbled and barked for attention.

I was pretty sure that the girl was the sister and that the bigger boys were her brothers. I could tell by their smell. Besides, I knew that this was how brothers behaved around sisters.

"Move over, Craig!" the bigger boy said, pushing the smaller one with his elbow.

"Don't shove, Ryan!" the younger one answered, pushing back.

The girl—Maggie Rose?—looked up at the woman. "Mom? Why is the little girl puppy so small?" she asked.

"She's the runt of the litter," the woman, Mom, answered. "It happens, honey. One puppy's born small, and then it's hard for her to get her fair share of food or milk, so she doesn't grow as quickly as the others."

The younger boy looked up from where he was letting White-Tail-Brother chew on his fingers.

"Runt—that's what we need to call you, Maggie Rose," he said with a laugh.

"Craig, that's enough," Mom told him sternly.

I sat and looked at the girl and the mother over my brothers' heads. I could see the girl's shoulders and head droop a little at her brother's words. She didn't reply.

"Boys, make some room for me," Mom said, and she reached over to open the gate in the wire wall.

As soon as the gate swung open, my brothers rushed into the hallway, piling into the boys' laps, jumping up to lick their faces and bite their hair. Craig and Ryan flopped down on the floor, laughing, and my brothers climbed over them just as they did to our mother when they wanted to play.

I stayed inside the cage. I would have liked to have smelled and tasted these new people close up and to find out if they had any food anywhere. But I knew about this kind of play. It always ended up with me getting squashed and stepped on.

"Oh, puppy, it's okay," Maggie Rose called softly. She knelt down, too, and held out her hands. "You can come. Come and play."

I liked her voice. I wanted to taste her hands some more. Carefully, I stepped around the wrestling boys and brothers and went to Maggie Rose's lap.

She didn't make any quick movements. She touched me gently. Her hands tasted just as good as before. I stuck my nose into the crease under her chin, where her skin was sweaty and delicious.

She giggled. "That tickles!" she said.

"I'm going to name this one Gunner!" said Ryan, holding up White-Tail-Brother so that his legs paddled in the air.

"This one's Butch!" said Craig, scratching Biggest-Brother's belly.

"How about Rodeo for the brown one?" Ryan said.

"No way. Max! Name him Max!"

"I'm going to name this one Lily," Maggie Rose said. She

put an arm around me, and I curled up into a ball in her lap. It felt as cozy as sleeping with my mother.

"Stupid name," Craig said.

"Why would anybody name a dog after a flower?" Ryan jeered.

"It's my favorite flower," Maggie Rose replied. Her voice was quiet but stubborn. "I'm naming her Lily."

Mom had walked away and was standing a few yards down the hallway, talking to a tall woman I hadn't met before. She had short black hair and boots on her feet. "Okay, boys, time to go," Mom called.

"Aw, Mom," Craig groaned.

"Soccer practice waits for no man, Craig. Or boy. Put the puppies back in the kennel."

"Mom, can I stay?" Maggie Rose pleaded. "I don't want to go to their soccer practice."

"They might get confused and use you as a ball, Runt!" Craig teased her.

Mom and the tall woman talked some more. "It's fine; I'll keep an eye on her," the tall woman agreed.

"Okay, Maggie Rose, you can stay," Mom called over. "Amelia's in charge. Help out and do what she tells you."

Maggie Rose grinned. She hugged me close to her face, which gave me a chance to push my head into her brown hair and sniff up the scents hiding in it.

The human brothers left. My dog brothers charged over to Maggie Rose, climbing into her lap, lapping at her face. Maggie Rose curled an arm around me to protect me from their assault.

She stood up, still holding me tight. Brothers plopped

off her lap and onto the floor. Maggie Rose herded them back to the kennel and shut the door on them.

They yipped and barked and put their paws up on the door. My mother, still lying at the back of the kennel, picked up her head and watched alertly, but she made no movements.

"I'm going to take you on an adventure, Lily," Maggie Rose said to me.

I liked her smell. I liked her voice. I liked her hands. But I didn't know where she was taking me as she carried me down the hallway, away from my kennel, away from my mother and brothers. Where were we going?

Chapter 2

As Maggie Rose carried me along the hallway, I saw that there were lots of kennels like the one where I lived with my mother and brothers. In some of the kennels, there were animals.

"Time to meet new friends," Maggie Rose told me.

She paused by a pen, and a dog inside came wagging to the wire gate. He was big and sleek and black, with a brown face and white around his muzzle. Maggie Rose held me down so that I could touch noses with him through the wire.

He was male! Like my brothers! But older than they were, even older than my mother. I never knew that there could be male dogs as big and old as this.

"This is Chester," Maggie Rose advised me. "His family had to move, and they couldn't take care of him anymore. We're going to find him a new family. That's what we do, Lily. We find families for animals who don't have a home. Like you!"

I didn't know what she was saying, but I liked her voice. I wiggled around to lick her nose.

She giggled and carried me on.

In the next pen, an animal about my size hesitated in the back corner. I stared—whatever this was, it wasn't a dog! "This is Oscar," Maggie Rose told me. "It's okay, Oscar. Lily won't hurt you. Come on out." She crouched down beside the gate.

Slowly the animal approached. He had sleek gray fur and wide yellow eyes and triangular ears that stood straight up on his head. I'd never seen ears like that! My own ears flopped down beside my face, like my mother's and my brothers'.

Maggie Rose tucked me under one arm and stuck the fingers of her other hand through the wire. Oscar came over and sniffed her. I thought he'd lick her fingers, which seemed like the proper thing to do, but instead he rubbed his face on them and made a low, rumbly noise. How strange!

"This is your first cat, isn't he, Lily?" Maggie Rose asked me. "Oscar loves people. Most strays are scared, but he's not. He's going to get adopted soon, I bet. Mom says he just has to be neutered first. That's so he can't have any babies. I love kittens, but there are already too many running loose in the world, Mom says. Okay, you can say hi, but be nice."

She let me come closer to the wire, and I inhaled Oscar's smell eagerly. It was so interesting to meet an animal who wasn't a dog! Oscar sniffed at me, too, and then he retreated back inside the cage, his tail up high and quivering nervously.

"Oscar isn't sure about dogs, even a little one like you," Maggie Rose said. She stood back up. "Come on, Lily."

In the next cage, I thought at first there was another cat. The animal inside was small like a cat, and he moved in the same kind of smooth, slinky way. But he had a longer body and shorter legs than Oscar, and he didn't smell like Oscar, either. He smelled fiercer. Wilder.

He came right up to the wire to stretch his neck up high and touch his small nose to mine. He had round black eyes that gleamed in the dim light and a black mask that covered half of his brown face.

"Hi, Freddie!" Maggie Rose greeted. "Freddie's not scared of anything, Lily. He's a ferret. He's just staying with us for the summer. In the fall, he's going back to Ryan's school. That's where he lives, in the science lab. He's got a big pen with ladders to climb and a hammock to sleep in, Ryan says."

I could see that Freddie had very strong white teeth underneath his twitching nose. He was interested in me and seemed friendly. A ferret was like a friendly version of a cat.

"Mom says ferrets aren't really pets, and they should be wild. But Freddie's never lived outside and he's too old to learn, so it's a good thing the science teacher takes care of him," Maggie Rose said.

I wondered what all her words meant. Freddie seemed to get bored with me, and he turned his back and dashed away, more quickly than I could run. He scrambled up a box and dove into a hole on the top. Moments later, his head poked out and he looked at Maggie Rose and me before pulling his head back in.

"I guess Freddie doesn't want company right now," Maggie Rose observed.

The next kennel she took me to had yet another new kind of animal! I was amazed. Before today, I knew that there were boy dogs and girl dogs, big dogs and small ones.

And of course people, too. Now I knew the smell and sight of cats and ferrets and—what was this thing?

Even smaller than Oscar or Freddie, it was round all over—a round head and a round body and round black eyes. The only thing that wasn't round was its tail—a huge, puffy thing that seemed to float up in the air behind its back, quivering and twitching with each movement.

It had one funny leg, all wrapped in something white that looked like cloth but that clunked loudly against the floor of the kennel. I'd never seen a leg like that!

Even with that funny leg, the creature moved quickly, in little darting movements that were very exciting to watch. I squirmed until Maggie Rose put me down, and then I scratched at the gate and whined a little.

I wanted this creature to come out or to let me in. I wanted to chase it. It needed to be chased.

But the gate was funny to touch—there was something smooth and clear over the wire so that my paw could not get through.

"No, Lily, Sammy can't come out," Maggie Rose said. "We're not supposed to play with him or touch him at all. He's a squirrel. He's not a pet. That's why his door is glass. We're just taking care of him until his leg is better, and then he'll go back to the park. He can't get used to people feeding him or petting him or dogs playing with him, or he won't be safe in the wild, see?"

I tipped my head and whined a little more. My tail wagged so hard it thumped against my rump. What was Maggie Rose talking about? Was she explaining how she was going to open up the gate and let me smell this little creature up close? And then chase and chase and chase?

"Better leave Sammy alone. Lily, come with me," Maggie Rose said. She scooped me up.

Oh well. If I couldn't play Chase with Sammy, at least I got to snuggle with Maggie Rose.

Maggie Rose took me along a hallway lined with great big sacks, each one bigger than my mother. They smelled marvelous. I wiggled, longing to get down and sniff a sack close up and maybe get my teeth into the paper that covered it and pull hard enough to make whatever was inside spill out. But Maggie Rose held me close.

"No, Lily. You're too young to eat regular dog food, anyway," she told me.

We were getting near a door, and I heard a frightened yip from the other side. I could tell there was a dog inside. She smelled older than I was, but younger than my mother. And she was terrified.

Lily pushed the door open, and I saw that the woman with short black hair was holding a small dog on a table and wrapping white cloth around one leg. I remembered that the woman's name was Amelia.

"Shut the door, Maggie Rose. I don't want this little thing to get loose," Amelia said.

The frightened dog was trembling under Amelia's hands. She was about my size, but she did not look like me. Instead of sleek, short fur in gray and white splotches, she had wiry black fur that stood out in all directions.

"Is she a stray?" Maggie Rose asked.

"Nope, just lost. Someone found her on the streets and brought her in. She's got a bite—I guess she tangled with something, maybe a raccoon. A little Yorkie like this is no match for a big, aggressive raccoon. She should have been kept indoors or in a fenced yard, but people don't always do that. But the good news is that she's microchipped, so I already called her family. They'll be in to get her right away. Her name's Missy. There, there, sweetie, don't be scared. Your leg's all fixed. Here you go."

Amelia bent over to put the little dog, Missy, on the floor. Missy sat down, hunched over, with her head low and her ears nearly flat against her skull. She was not happy to be off the table and down on the floor. She was still frightened.

"Say hi, Lily," Maggie Rose told me. She set me down on the floor, too.

I studied Missy. She was not ready to play. If I bounded up to her like my brothers did to me, she might run away. She might even snap at me—she looked and smelled scared enough to do it.

But there wasn't anything to be scared of here. There was just Maggie Rose, who was nice, and Amelia, who was probably nice, too—because Maggie Rose was talking to her and smiling and comfortable in her presence. If Maggie Rose felt okay with Amelia, Amelia was okay with me.

And there was me. I wasn't scary; I was a puppy! I went a little closer to Missy and wagged my tail. I kept my head and ears up, but not so high that she'd think I wanted to boss her around. I didn't want to boss her. I just wanted to play with her.

I moved a little closer.

Missy picked her head up a bit.

I stopped and waited.

Missy's ears lifted.

I went closer and sniffed Missy all over. She still smelled

scared, but not as scared as before. She smelled like Amelia's hands, and the white bandage on her leg had a strange, sharp odor that I did not like. But Missy's fur held a lot of very interesting scents. It smelled a bit like Maggie Rose's shoes, with scents of a place I had never been. Someplace out there bigger than my kennel, someplace with dirt and air and wind and lots and lots of animals and people.

Later, I would learn that this smell was called Outside, or Out.

Missy sniffed me back. She got up and shook herself. I shook, too, just to be friendly. Then Missy pushed at me a little with her nose. I pushed back. I nibbled at her face. She shook herself and pulled away. I flopped over on my back, paws in the air. Missy limped over and put her good paw across my belly.

I wiggled. She jumped.

In a moment, we were wrestling.

I knew to go easy with Missy, because her leg still hurt her. But she did not let that stop her. It was fun playing with a dog my size instead of three bigger brothers. Missy knew when to stop, too. When she stepped on my ear and I yipped, she stepped off right away.

I liked Missy!

"Oh, look!" I heard Maggie Rose say. "Lily got Missy to play. She's not so scared now."

"Lily? Is that the puppy's name now? Good work, Lily," Amelia praised with a smile.

Not long after that, I heard a door open somewhere, and in a moment a woman rushed into the room. A boy Maggie Rose's age was behind her.

"Oh, Missy!" the woman wailed.

Missy stopped licking my face to bound to the woman's feet. The woman, tears flowing down her cheeks, snatched her up and hugged her and held her close. "I was frantic! I just looked around and she was gone. It's been two days!" she said.

Missy was not scared at all now. Missy was very, very happy.

This weeping woman was Missy's person, I realized with a jolt of understanding. That's why Missy was so happy.

I looked at Maggie Rose. I had a person, too! Maggie Rose was my person, my very own girl. We belonged together, the way Missy belonged to the crying lady.

The woman and Amelia talked, and Amelia gave the woman some papers and the woman gave them back. My girl, Maggie Rose, sat down on the floor to let me climb into her lap. I was a little tired and curled up for a rest.

The boy came over and knelt down beside us. "Can I pet her?" he asked. He had a soft, shy voice.

"Sure," Maggie Rose said, and the boy reached out to rub my ears. Very nice.

"I'm glad you got your dog back," my girl told him.

"She's my mom's dog, really," the boy said. "But I'm glad, too. What kind is your dog?"

"Not really mine," Maggie Rose said. Her voice sounded a little sad, and I wondered why. I had a girl, and she had a puppy. No reason to be sad. "She's waiting for adoption. Her mom and brothers, too. The mom's a pit bull, so Lily's a pit mix."

"She's cute," the boy said. "She really likes you."

Maggie Rose nodded.

After a while, the boy and the woman with wet cheeks

left with Missy. Too bad. I would have liked to have played some more. Maggie Rose kept petting me, so I stayed in her lap, growing sleepier and sleepier.

"Going to take Lily back to her mom?" Amelia asked.

Maggie Rose didn't move. "I want her to be mine," she said, looking up at Amelia. "My own dog."

Amelia sighed. "Maggie Rose," she said gently. "You know that won't work. You know why."

My girl held me close to her face. I was limp with sleepiness and didn't stir in her hands.

"Yes, it will," Maggie Rose whispered to me.

Chapter 3

Maggie Rose settled me down again in her lap, and I had a nice snooze there. When I woke up, it was because I heard a door slam shut.

"Hi, Jessica, we're in here!" Amelia called out.

I stretched and yawned in my girl's lap and curled up again, ready to sleep some more as the tall woman I'd seen before came in. I remembered that Maggie Rose called her Mom.

"Put the little pup back in her kennel," Mom told Maggie Rose. "The boys are waiting in the car. We need to go."

Maggie Rose didn't stir. She put her hands around me. It reminded me of the way my mother would curl her body around mine while I slept.

"I want to keep Lily," my girl declared. Her voice was soft. "I want to take her home."

"Oh no," Mom replied with a long sigh. "Maggie Rose, you know we can't do that."

Amelia had a sad smile on her face as she looked back and forth between Maggie Rose and Mom.

"I'll take care of her," Maggie Rose insisted. "She'll be my dog. I'll do all the work."

Mom sighed again, shaking her head. "For the summer, I'm sure you would. What about when you go to school in the fall? And I'm at work here? Who's going to look after Lily then?"

Maggie Rose gazed up at Mom imploringly. "Can't she come here with you? While you're working?" she asked.

Amelia looked at Mom. Mom looked at Amelia. Now they both seemed sad.

"Maggie Rose," said Amelia gently. "We can't do that. We're a rescue organization. We save animals and find homes for them. We don't keep the animals ourselves. And there's a good reason for that."

Now my girl was sad! I could feel it in her body. I snuggled closer, wondering what was troubling her. I wanted to help. Making people less sad was something a puppy should be very good at, I decided.

Amelia crouched down to look at Maggie Rose. "I can tell you really care about Lily. But we only have room for a few animals here. If Lily stays, then there's one less place for a rescue animal. That's not fair to all the animals who need us."

I rolled onto my back and stuck my legs in the air—now *this* should make anyone happy!

"But Lily could help," Maggie Rose insisted. The hope was draining out of her voice. "She likes the other animals. She helped with Missy."

Amelia sat back a little. "Well, that's true. Lily did help Missy calm down. But that doesn't change the facts, hon. We do the most good when we place animals into homes, and that's what we're going to do with Lily. In another week, she'll be ready to leave her mommy, and we'll find her a good family who'll love her as much as you do."

Time for some drastic action. I rolled onto my feet,

raised my paws, and tried to lick my girl on the chin. Instead of laughing, though, she just turned her head away.

"Maggie Rose," Mom said. "Put Lily back in her kennel and come with me. You can visit her every day this week—that's okay, isn't it, Amelia?"

"Sure thing," Amelia agreed, getting up. "It's great to get the puppies used to being with kids. It helps them adjust to their new homes."

"We're going home now, Maggie Rose." Mom patted my girl's shoulder, but her voice was firm. "Tell Lily good-bye."

I could tell that my girl was still sad, even though I was frantically licking her cheeks as she carried me back to my kennel and put me inside in the midst of a pack of yelping, jumping brothers. What was going on? Why couldn't I kiss her and cuddle her into happiness?

"Don't worry, Lily," Maggie Rose whispered to me. "I'll never let you go. You're going to stay with me."

I could hear good-bye in her voice. I licked Maggie Rose's fingers to tell her I was not done trying to make her happy, but she stood and walked away.

I hurried over to my mother. I was ready for another nap after such an adventure outside my pen. Meeting other dogs and a cat and that long, funny ferret . . . playing with Missy . . . cuddling with Maggie Rose. It had all been very exciting, but it was time for a good long rest.

As I drifted off into a nice, warm sleep, I thought about what I now saw as my job—making Maggie Rose happy, no matter what was making her unhappy. I knew that as long as we kept seeing each other every day, I would succeed!

Sure enough, Maggie Rose came back every day! I soon knew her scent and the sound of her footsteps, and I'd be waiting at the gate when she arrived, my tail wagging hard enough to make my entire rump wiggle. My girl would take me out and hug me and pet me. She'd sit on the floor and let me climb in her lap and lick her chin and sniff at her clothes, which were always full of all the interesting odors she brought with her.

I wished I could go wherever my girl went and discover where all these scents came from. Her tennis shoes held the best odors of all. Plus the laces were so good for pulling on.

I loved Maggie Rose's shoes. I loved Maggie Rose.

And she loved me, yet something was still going on with her. I could make her giggle, and she covered me with as many kisses as I gave her, but deep inside something was still making her sad. What she needed to do, I decided, was come live with me here, where I could work on keeping her giggling all day and night. She could sleep between my mother and me.

Sometimes my girl's big brothers came, too. "Hey, Runt. Still playing with the flower dog, Runt?" Ryan, the tallest one, asked one day as I was trying to pull a rope toy out of Maggie Rose's hand. "Perfect dog for you. Look, she's so tiny and weak, she can't even win at tug-of-war!"

Maggie Rose's shoulders hunched stubbornly. "There's nothing wrong with being little," she answered.

Ryan snorted. "Oh, I know, I used to be little, too, when I was a *baby*. Bye, Runt." He went on down the hall.

"There's nothing wrong with being little," my girl repeated softly to me. "Better to be little and nice than big and mean, Lily. Right?"

She let go of the rope toy, so I won! I gripped it in my teeth and shook it hard. Then I ran back to her and plopped the damp bit of rope in her lap so we could play again.

While I tugged, I heard a door open somewhere. Footsteps approached. New people were arriving! I leaped into Maggie Rose's lap so I could check them out from a safe place.

Mom came down the hall, leading another woman, a man, and a boy who was bigger than Maggie Rose but smaller than Ryan. "These are wonderful, active dogs," Mom was saying as they walked. "And they're fine with children. I bring my own kids here to play with the pups regularly to socialize them. They're going to be great family dogs."

Mom and the pack of people she was leading stopped by our kennel. Maggie Rose scooted to one side to give them room. She put both hands around me, and I felt her body tense. Then, suddenly, she grabbed the front of her T-shirt and pulled its soft folds completely over me.

I was inside my girl's shirt, held against her skin. I wiggled in surprise. Was this a new game? Her heart was pounding, and now she wasn't just unhappy—she was afraid!

I knew there was something I should be doing to help her, because I was her puppy, but what? I could see Maggie Rose's chin up through a small hole at the top of the shirt—should I try to climb up there?

I heard my brothers yip inside the pen, the wire gate rattling as they jumped up to put their paws against it.

"Oh, Mom, the spotted one! I want the spotted one!" I heard one of the new boys say.

I felt Maggie Rose relax suddenly. Glad whatever it was had stopped being scary, I seized a fold of her T-shirt in my teeth and shook it. Then I wrestled with it.

"Here, Lily," Maggie Rose whispered to me. She picked up the hem of her shirt so I could squirm back out into the light.

That was a strange game. I liked Tug the Rope better.

The new boy had picked up Biggest-Brother and was holding him under his chin. Biggest-Brother was wiggling around to lick the boy's neck, just as I liked to do with Maggie Rose.

The new woman and man were smiling as they watched.

"This one. This one!" the boy insisted, hugging Biggest-Brother close.

"Okay, then. You've already filled out an application, and we've checked your references, so we're all set!" Mom said.

"We can take him now?" the new woman asked. "We've got a crate in the car."

"Perfect." Mom smiled.

The boy carried Biggest-Brother away down the hall. I figured he must be going on an adventure, the kind Maggie Rose sometimes took me on. Oscar meowed as they went past, and Freddie the ferret dashed up to his gate to see what was happening and then dove back into his den.

Mom lingered behind to gaze down at Maggie Rose.

"You see, hon? See how happy they were?" she asked gently. "That's how this works."

My girl didn't answer. She put me back in my pen after a final cuddle and kiss. Her sadness was out in the open again. I sat and stared up at her, wondering if I should have tried to stay under the T-shirt longer.

Later that day, I realized something very strange happened: Biggest-Brother did not come back.

I dodged away from White-Tail-Brother, who wanted to sit on me, and nipped at Brown-Brother's nose so that he'd keep his distance. Then I went to my mother, who was sitting up in her corner, watching the gate alertly.

She barked once, sharply. It meant, "Come here!"

I pressed against her side. My brothers stopped splashing in the water bowl and went to her, too.

But Biggest-Brother did not come. Not ever again. He was gone.

Over the next few days, the same thing happened again. And *again!* New people came and talked and were happy, and when they left they took a puppy. Brown-Brother went with a man and three girls who all talked at once. White-Tail-Brother was carried away in the arms of a tall young woman wearing jeans and boots and a wide, wide smile.

Maggie Rose was playing with me each time this happened. She kept me in her lap the whole time, which made me feel better when the people left with a brother. Maggie Rose was safety, just like my mother. She had strong arms and a warm lap, and I could feel the love in her hands and hear it in her voice. I knew she would not let anyone take me away. I just wished I could be a better puppy for her so she wouldn't be so sad.

The day after White-Tail-Brother left, Maggie Rose came to visit with a new scent on her hands. It smelled like Oscar the cat, except there were two of them!

"Oh, Lily, the new kittens are so cute!" my girl told me. "I bet you'd like to see them. You can play together!"

"No way, Maggie Rose," Amelia said from out in the hallway. She was brushing at the floor with a broom.

"Why not?" Maggie Rose asked, looking up from where she was sitting on the floor with me. "They'd have fun."

"It's not worth the risk," Amelia answered. "Somebody could get hurt."

"But Lily wouldn't hurt a kitten," Maggie Rose responded indignantly. "Remember how careful she was with Missy?"

"Maybe she wouldn't mean to. But puppies and kittens play very differently, and it would be easy for one of them to get scared and lash out. Remember when Craig let Freddie the ferret out of his cage when a cat was loose? I was terrified that one of them would bite the other. We have to keep the animals separate to keep them safe."

Amelia swept her way down the hall, and Maggie Rose brought out a rubber ring for me to gnaw on. But after a while, Mom called her, and she hugged me and kissed me and went away.

Then it was just my mother and me all alone in our kennel. I had always thought I had too many brothers, but lately I was thinking that it was actually worse to have no brothers at all. My mother did not want to play, and my girl was gone. I was bored and missed my littermates, and most of all, I missed Maggie Rose.

So when a new man came to the gate, I was happy to greet him.

Amelia was with him, and she opened up the gate so that I could come out. "Here's the last puppy left from this litter," she said. "Her name is Lily."

My mother hung back, but I was excited to make a new friend. I trotted over at once and sniffed his shoes. Shoes were always so fascinating.

Big hands came down and scooped me up, and the man held me up so that I could see his face. He had a soft shirt that smelled a little like Oscar the cat, and he also had fur on his face. I'd never seen a human with fur on his face! I wiggled in close to sniff it and lick it. It smelled of something sweet and soapy, and also of scrambled eggs and coffee and sugar.

"She's tiny, but she's not shy, is she?" the man said, laughing.

"One of our volunteers has worked very hard on socializing her," Amelia said, and there was something just a little bit sad in her voice. I cocked my ear at her. Why was *she* sad? Weren't we all making friends?

I was beginning to worry that I wasn't very good at being a puppy. Otherwise, why couldn't I cheer anybody up?

"She's perfect! Can I have her?" the man asked. *He* seemed happy, anyway.

"Well, we ask that everyone use the application process," Amelia said. "And there's an interview with our director, and we check references. But yes, if you want Lily, I'm sure that can be arranged."

The man held me out a little from his face so that he could look at me all over.

"You're going to be my dog!" he told me. "Would you like that? Want to come home with me?"

I wondered what he was talking about. And when was Maggie Rose going to come back? She'd probably like to meet my new friend. We could all be friends together.

Chapter 4

The day after I'd met my new friend, my girl returned. I was so happy to greet her! I licked her face, remembering the happy man with fur on his cheeks and chin. Maybe if Maggie Rose grew fur on her face, she would be as easy to cheer up! She picked me up and tucked me under her arm and then carried me into the hallway.

I squirmed a little. I didn't really mind her carrying me, but it was more fun to be on the floor with her. We couldn't play a lot of games when I was in her arms.

I could feel that Maggie Rose was nervous. I licked her arm so she'd know I was there to take care of her.

"Come on, Lily," she whispered. "Mom and Amelia are having a meeting, and nobody else is working in the shelter right now."

She took me past Chester's cage. Freddie the ferret ran up to the gate of his kennel to watch us go past and made a funny chattering noise that was not a bark or a growl or a whimper.

At the next cage, Maggie Rose stopped. She put me down on the ground. I pressed my nose up to the gate.

I smelled a familiar smell.

There were two cats inside. Young ones. Small. A boy and a girl. I'd smelled them before, on my girl's shirt. Now they were right here in front of me!

One had gray stripes. The other had blotchy spots all over in yellowish and white and black. Stripes was the boy. Blotchy was the girl. Stripes crept back into a box with his wide eyes on me, but Blotchy came over to the gate to touch noses. Her fur bristled out from her body a little, and I could smell that she was nervous. I wagged to let her know that I was friendly.

"Okay, guys?" my girl whispered. "Okay!"

She opened the pen.

I did not charge straight in. I remembered how I did not like it when my brothers did that. They'd run right at me and bowl me over before I was ready to play.

Instead, I walked slowly up to Blotchy. She opened her mouth wide. I could see her sharp white teeth.

"Oh," Maggie Rose whispered nervously. "Maybe . . ."

I yawned, too, just like Blotchy. Then I sat down and stretched my neck to sniff at Blotchy's face. Her breath smelled very interesting! Meaty and fishy! I liked it! My tail wagged harder.

Blotchy sniffed back, and then suddenly she pushed her face hard against my cheek. It almost shoved me right over! How could such a tiny thing push so hard?

She did it again, with the other side of her face. A funny rumbling sound came from deep in her throat. But it was not a growl. I could tell she was friendly.

I licked her face. She shook her head in surprise. Now her fur was wet.

Then something sharp stabbed at my tail!

I yelped and spun around. Behind me, Stripes leaped away on stiff legs. He'd crept up behind me and pounced on my tail!

Now he was running away!

Obviously, he wanted to play Chase Me! I knew about Chase Me. My brothers had played it all the time.

He should have asked before just jumping on my tail like that, but it was all right. I was ready to play!

I chased Stripes back to his box, and he jumped up on top of it and let out a funny sound from a wide-open mouth—a hiss. What strange noises cats made.

Blotchy crouched down low, wiggled her rump, and pounced at me, grabbing my back foot with her claws.

Oh! Wrestling? We were playing Wrestling now?

I flopped down on Blotchy and rolled over. She batted at my ear. I mouthed at her leg. But I was careful not to bite, and she kept her claws gentle. They pricked my leg, but they didn't hurt.

She understood Wrestling.

Stripes leaped down from his box and landed on Blotchy's rump, and she sprang up and whirled around in midair. (I wished I could do that!) She chased her brother around the kennel, and I helped out by following her, until we all ended up in a heap in the middle of the kennel and Blotchy suddenly started washing my ears and head with her strong, raspy pink tongue.

Did she think she was my mother?

Maggie Rose had both hands over her mouth to stifle her laughter, but it still slipped out in giggles around her fingers. "Lily, you're so sweet!" she said as I shook my head so that Blotchy would stop licking me. "Come on. Maybe that's enough for one day."

She picked me up and carried me out of the kennel. Blotchy switched to washing Stripes's face until he batted her on the nose and darted over to get a drink from the water bowl.

Maggie Rose shut the gate to the kittens' kennel. Then she set me down in front of the cage next door.

Freddie the ferret was already standing by the gate, his tiny nose quivering, his whole long, slender body alert.

"Lily, don't ever tell anybody about this," my girl said to me, very softly.

She opened the gate.

For half a second, Freddie and I stared at each other with no wire between us.

Then Freddie sprang out. He didn't run anything like my brothers with their big clumsy paws, or like Blotchy and Stripes with their feather-light movements. Freddie *flowed*. He was quick and smooth, dashing past me, racing along the rows of cages. Chester barked, startled. Oscar meowed. Stripes and Blotchy mewed.

I chased.

Of course that's what we were doing, wasn't it? We were playing Chase Me! Just like the kittens, Freddie didn't quite know the rules. He didn't know to bow down or to look back over his shoulder to tell me to follow.

But I knew to run after him anyway. My feet wanted to. Anything that moved that quickly *needed* to be chased!

I couldn't get close to him! It was impossible. Freddie went faster and faster. Maggie Rose was starting to get nervous; I could tell. She wanted me to catch Freddie. I would do it!

Suddenly, Freddie doubled back on his own tracks. One second he was racing forward; the next he was going in the other direction! I couldn't stop that fast. I toppled forward

onto my nose. Freddie stopped at Chester's cage and chittered through the bars at him. Chester barked urgently. He wanted to play Chase Me, too. He wanted it very badly.

I sat up, shaking my head, and got ready to chase Freddie some more. He turned in a circle in front of Chester's cage, almost as if he were teasing the big dog. I ran forward and jumped on the ferret. He couldn't get away this time!

We rolled over and over. Freddie nipped me on my nose. It didn't hurt much, though. And I was having too good of a time to stop.

I jumped up and seized Freddie by the neck. Maggie Rose let out a little gasp. "Lily!" she cried out.

I wanted to reassure Maggie Rose, but I was busy. I pulled Freddie down the hallway. His long white body was limp in my mouth, as if he were a puppy and I were a mother dog.

"Lily, no!" Maggie Rose called out.

I looked up at her in surprise, and Freddie wiggled out of my mouth. My turn to run! His turn to chase!

But the ferret surprised me. He didn't chase after me. Instead, he jumped up on the wire gate of the cage that held Stripes and Blotchy, clinging to it with his claws.

Hey! That wasn't fair! I couldn't chase him up there!

Freddie swarmed up the door easily and ran across the top of the cage. I put my paws up on the door of the cage and barked. Now Stripes and Blotchy were mewing at me!

Freddie paused on top of the cage. He looked at me over his shoulder. And then he wiggled down behind the cage, slipping easily into a crack between it and the wall behind it.

He was gone. I couldn't see him anymore.

"Oh no!" Maggie Rose gasped. "Oh no. Freddie! Freddie! Come back! Please come back!"

I didn't understand what was going on. Where was Freddie? Was playtime over?

Maggie Rose ran to the cage that held Stripes and Blotchy. She grabbed hold of the wire door and pulled. But the crate was connected to the cage on each side, and the whole row together was too heavy for my girl to move.

She was breathing in quick gasps and sniffing hard. I could sense her fear and worry. Something was very wrong! But I didn't know what it was.

I ran to Maggie Rose's feet and whimpered to tell her that I was worried, too. We could be worried together.

"Oh, Lily!" she cried. "This is all my fault. What if he gets stuck back there? What if he can't get out?"

My girl sat down and grabbed me. She plopped me into her lap. Her hands were squeezing me a little too tightly, but I didn't mind very much. I could tell she needed me.

"Oh, Lily, there's a pipe back there that leads outside! I saw it once. I asked Mom about it. Ferrets love to explore. What if Freddie thinks it's a tunnel and crawls into it? He could end up outside. And he doesn't know how to live outside! Freddie might die, Lily!"

The sadness and fear were so strong coming off my girl I felt compelled to do something. I wiggled off her lap and hurried over to the row of cages. If I went around behind them, I could see the crack between the cages and the wall.

Freddie was skinnier than I was. I couldn't get my body into that crack. I could barely get my nose in.

I could smell Freddie in there. I whined a little. When I whined to my mother, she always came to find me. Maybe Freddie would do the same thing.

Chapter 5

Something tickled my nose. Whiskers! Small black eyes blinked at me from the darkness between the cages and the wall.

I backed up. Freddie wiggled out from the crack. I sniffed him. He smelled dusty.

More Chase Me?

"Oh, Lily, good dog," Maggie Rose whispered. "Just come here so Freddie will follow you. Lily, come. Lily, please. Lily, come and see me."

Maggie Rose was saying my name a lot. I decided that she must need me. I hurried to her and licked the hands she was holding out.

Freddie scampered behind me. I was right! He was ready to run after me now!

But Maggie Rose seemed to think that playtime was at an end. She reached out for Freddie and snatched him up. He chattered at me and tried to twist himself out of my girl's hands, but she held him tightly and carried him to his cage. She put him in and shut the door.

Then she sat down on the floor and trembled. I ran to her and climbed into her lap. I didn't know why we couldn't play more, but Maggie Rose obviously needed a puppy right now, needed me more than ever. I pushed at her hands with my nose until she remembered to pet me. I could feel her calming down as she stroked my back and rubbed my neck. There, I was getting better at helping her! The fear was going away. Now I just needed to fix her unhappiness!

After Maggie Rose stopped shaking, she picked me up and carried me into my own kennel. She sat down next to my mother. It was very nice. Maggie Rose, my mother, and me.

"I'll never, never do that again, Lily," she said softly. "Oh, Lily. I don't know what I will do when they take you away from me."

After a little bit, my girl lay down on the carpet where my mother usually slept. Her face was wet. My mother sniffed at Maggie Rose and gently licked her cheek.

It reminded me of how my mother used to lick me when I was very small. Then she would pick me up and carry me somewhere by the skin on the back of my neck, the way I had just been carrying Freddie. Her mouth was so very gentle when she did this that I was never afraid. I knew she was taking me somewhere safe. That's what mothers do.

I licked my girl's cheek, too. The wetness tasted salty.

Then I wiggled myself under my girl's chin, and my mother lay down along my girl's back. Maggie Rose's breathing got slower and slower. We all took a nice nap together. It was the best nap I ever had.

When I woke up, Mom was standing there, looking down at the three of us. She was smiling, but she looked sad, too. She sat down on the floor and gently touched Maggie Rose's arm.

Maggie Rose stirred and opened her eyes.

"Hello, sweetie," Mom said. "Nice sleep?"

Maggie Rose nodded. She sat up but kept me in her lap.

"Honey," Mom said after a few moments. "I know you love this little dog. But you've played with lots of dogs in the shelter, and you've always been happy when they've gotten adopted. Why is Lily so different?"

Maggie Rose looked down at me. I wagged.

"Because she's like me," she said in a voice so soft Mom had to lean a little closer to hear it.

"Like you?" Mom asked. Her voice was as gentle as my mother's tongue. Maybe that's how human mothers lick their young ones—with words.

"We're both runts," Maggie Rose explained.

"Oh, honey," her mom answered.

"We are, Mom. I'm the shortest girl in my class at school, and Lily is the littlest one in the litter. And she has big brothers, too. Just like me."

"I see," Mom said, nodding.

"And I just . . . love her, Mom. I just do. And she loves me."

Mom nodded again. "I can see that. But, honey, you have to believe me when I tell you this—you'll love other dogs in your life. Lily is very special, but all dogs are special. And I have good news. We just finished processing an application, and Lily's mother is being adopted! Isn't that wonderful? I'm going to take her to her new home right now."

"But Lily will be all alone," Maggie Rose said.

"No, hon, she'll have you," Mom answered, still in that gentle voice. "And then she'll have a family of her own very soon."

Mom took out a leash and clipped it onto my mother's

collar. Then she stood up and tugged on the leash gently.

"Come, sweetie," she said. "Come with me. You're going to your new forever home."

My mother got up and shook herself. She looked at me, still in Maggie Rose's lap. Then she followed Mom out of the kennel. Mom shut the door behind her.

And with that, my mother was gone.

I was very confused. I wiggled out of my girl's lap and went to the door and sniffed. I could tell my mother's scent was following her farther and farther away.

I whined. She always came when I whined.

But this time she did not come.

I whined again, louder. Maybe she hadn't heard me the first time.

"Oh, Lily!" Maggie Rose said.

She picked me up and held me close. She petted me and talked to me. Her cheeks were wet again, and they had that salty taste. She was so, so sad. She rocked me gently back and forth.

"It'll be okay. It'll be okay," she told me.

I was glad that Maggie Rose was close. But I wished my mother were there, too.

After a while, Mom returned and spoke to Maggie Rose. "Time to go, sweetie."

It had been a strange day—fun, then scary, then cozy, then sad. I hoped it would be fun again soon. I hoped my mother would come back and she and Maggie Rose and I could be together. Maybe we'd take another nap.

Amelia turned out most of the lights and left. It was dark. It was very quiet. It was lonely.

I could smell Freddie and Chester and Stripes and

Blotchy. I could smell my brothers, although their scent was starting to fade. I could smell my mother.

All by myself, I lay on the carpet that smelled like my family. I whined and whimpered, but no one came to be with me.

It was the worst night of my life.

In the morning, lights popped on, and Amelia brought me food in bowls and fresh water. I was so happy to see her that I charged up to her, licking her pants and shoes and panting anxiously up into her face and trying to let her know how awful, how very awful, the night had been. Where was my mother? Where was Maggie Rose? Where was everybody?

"There, there, Lily!" Amelia petted me gently. "It's going to be okay. It won't be long now."

Later, after breakfast, my girl came. Maggie Rose! I flung myself at her, and she held me until all the loneliness of the night before had been forgotten.

My mother was still gone. My brothers were still gone. But Maggie Rose was here. And I loved Maggie Rose. As long as we were together, I would not be lonely.

Mom came to the gate of our kennel and stood there, looking in.

"I have some news, Maggie Rose," she said.

Maggie Rose looked up hopefully.

"We've found a home for Lily," she said. "I'll be taking her there tomorrow."

My girl's smile fell away. The sadness, which was always

lurking in her like a shadow, came forward and took over her mood completely.

Mom came into the kennel and tried to hug her and talk to her in those words that were like a mother dog licking her puppy, but Maggie Rose did not want to be held. She did not want words.

At last Mom patted her shoulder and left.

Maggie Rose held me and cried and cried. I did my best to help. I licked her chin and her salty face. I nuzzled my head under her arm so I'd be as close to her as I could. I told her without words that I was her dog, and she didn't need to be so sad when I was with her.

But none of it helped. All that day, Maggie Rose was as sad as I'd been all night long.

Why couldn't I make her happy?

Chapter 6

At last Maggie Rose left with Mom, and I spent another night all alone. Another one! When would this end?

Thank goodness my girl came to see me early in the morning. She was still sad, though! I could not understand it. It made sense to be sad when we were apart. But why when we were together?

I tried rolling on my back and racing around in circles and jumping up to lick her face—all the puppy tricks I had. None of it seemed to work.

My girl slipped a collar around my neck and attached a leash to it. Then she took me into the hallway.

But we didn't stop and play there, as I'd expected. Maggie Rose led me through a door, one I'd never been through before.

I was amazed. There was a huge sky overhead and grass underfoot. Grass! It smelled fresh and alive and like all the things that had walked on it and peed on it. It had bugs and sticks hidden in it. And underneath it was rich, fragrant dirt.

Then Maggie Rose picked me up. I was not done sniffing and digging and exploring, but I was excited to see where we were going next. My girl held me tightly and slid into a big van. She sat in the back seat. Mom was up front, sitting behind a big wheel that she held with her hands.

The van smelled even more interesting than the dirt!

So many animals had been here. My mother! My mother had been in this van! I squirmed out of Maggie Rose's arms and sniffed the seats. I sniffed the floor that was covered in rough carpet. I could smell that my mother had been nervous, but not too scared. Where had she gone?

And others from my dog family had been here. I even thought I caught a faint whiff of White-Tail-Brother buried deep in the cushions of the seat where Maggie Rose was sitting. Chester had definitely also been here, and not too long ago.

The van suddenly gave a lurch, and I staggered. Maggie Rose picked me up and held me on her lap.

We were moving!

I braced my back feet on Maggie Rose's lap and my front feet on a slippery glass window and stared outside in amazement. Things were flying past us faster than I could run—trees and other cars, signs and posts and wires, bushes and buildings, people walking. Some of the people had dogs with them. I had never known that the world was so big and so busy and so full!

My girl pressed a button, and the window moved a bit. Cool air rushed in through a gap between the top of the window and its frame, packed so full of smells that I almost peed with excitement. I pressed my nose to the gap and sniffed and sniffed and sniffed.

There was something familiar about the wonderful mix of odors blowing in. When had I smelled something like that before? Oh yes, when I'd lived with my mother and brothers before the shelter. That had been a cold, dark time, but interesting smells like this had wafted past my nose most days. Then we'd gone to the shelter, and there we'd mostly been able to smell ourselves, plus the other animals and people like Maggie Rose and Mom and Amelia.

But now! Now I had Maggie Rose to snuggle with and all the wonderful odors to fill my nose. My tail whapped back and forth, swatting Maggie Rose's chest and arms. This was amazing! This was the best adventure ever!

But Maggie Rose didn't seem to think so. I could still feel her sadness soaking into me.

From her seat up front, Mom was talking. "This is going to be a wonderful home for Lily. The man who's adopting her is a radio disc jockey, and that means he's only at work for a couple of hours in the morning. The rest of the time he's home and can stay with Lily. She'll have plenty of company. He even thinks he could bring her to the radio station when she's a little older. She'll have a great life."

Maggie Rose put her head down and buried her face in my fur. She didn't answer. I turned my attention to my purpose, which was to puppy-away my girl's sadness. I dug my head in under hers and pushed, licking her face.

It wasn't working.

Suddenly, a funny burst of music came from the seat next to Mom. I never knew that vans made music! My ears perked up to hear it. Mom turned the wheel, and the van moved to the side of the road and stopped. Mom put a small black box to her ear. "Hello?"

Then Mom talked for a while more. She was quiet for a bit, nodding, and then she started talking again. People do strange stuff sometimes, and all a puppy can do is wait for things to make sense again.

Then Mom put the black box down.

"We need to make a detour, Maggie Rose," she said. "That was Amelia. She just got a call. There's a duplex near here where the people moved out more than a month ago. The landlord just went in to clean out the vacant apartment and found a bunch of cats living there. Probably a mom with kittens. It's that time of year. We'll have to go and get them. It shouldn't take too long."

Maggie Rose snuggled her face back into my fur again.

"I wish it would take forever," she whispered to me mournfully. "Then we could stay together, Lily."

The van rolled along for a while longer and then stopped. Maggie Rose slid out, still holding me. Mom got out, too. She went to the back of the van, opened up a door, and took out two plastic boxes with wire gates on the front. They looked like small kennels, but with handles on the top so that they could be carried.

There was a building nearby with two front doors. A man came out of one of those doors. He closed the door behind him, but I heard barking. I sniffed. Dogs lived behind that door. Two of them.

"Thanks for coming," the man said. He wore a grubby shirt and a pair of jeans with dirt ground into the knees. "I haven't been into the place since the last tenants left. This morning I was going to get it cleaned up and ready for the new people, and in one of the bedrooms upstairs I found a bunch of cats! Couldn't believe it!"

"Cats or kittens?" Mom asked.

The man shrugged. "Beats me. I didn't look too closely, just shut the door so they couldn't get out. I don't know about cats. I've got dogs. Cats and dogs don't get along, ever."

"That's not true," Maggie Rose objected softly. "Lily loves cats. Kittens, too. She gets along with everybody."

The man shrugged again. "Well, I wouldn't take a puppy in there. Want me to keep yours while you take care of the cats?"

Maggie Rose hugged me more tightly. "No!" she said firmly.

Mom sighed. "It'll be all right. Maggie Rose, come with me. But keep a hold on Lily."

We went into the other door, which did not have dogs behind it. Mom walked ahead, carrying her small kennels. Maggie Rose followed behind her, carrying me.

Once we were inside the door, Mom shut it behind us. At once, I could smell cats.

Cats! When I played with cats, Maggie Rose giggled. I knew how to make her happy!

I wiggled until my girl set me down. The floor was made of slippery wood. I didn't let that stop me, though. I scrambled and slid from corner to corner, sniffing hard. Where were those cats?

Mom and my girl kept walking, so I scampered to keep up. Then I stopped dead.

Stairs.

Mom stepped on the first stair, then the second, then the third, moving up. Maggie Rose followed. I'd never seen people do anything like that!

Well, I would just have to follow. The first stair was tall! Almost as tall as I was! It was hard work to jump up and put my front feet on its surface. I hoped they wouldn't all be like this!

Then I tried to heave my back feet up behind me.

Impossible! My back feet slipped off the stair, and my front feet could not hold on. I scrabbled at the wood with my claws before I flopped back to the floor.

Maggie Rose and Mom were already nearly at the top. There were doors up there, and new rooms, and the smell of cats was even stronger.

I yipped in frustration, and my girl turned around.

"Oh, Lily!" she exclaimed. She came down to get me.

It felt so, so good to be back in her arms. I hoped I would never again be separated from Maggie Rose.

Mom was standing in front of a closed door. The smell of cats wafted out from under it. They were inside there! Lots of them, young ones. We were going to have such fun.

"Keep hold of Lily," said Mom, pulling a pair of thick leather gloves over her hands. They went up to her elbows.

I wagged to hear my name and because I was going to get to play with kittens again very soon. Mom opened the door.

I was so excited that I could not stay in my girl's arms. I wiggled and squirmed and pushed with my back feet. Maggie Rose gasped with alarm and shifted her grip, but I gave one last twist and jumped to the floor.

Kitties!

Maggie Rose fell to her knees, grabbing for me, but she was too late. I was already running straight into the room where I knew the cats were waiting for me.

Maybe a puppy alone wasn't enough to lift her sadness, but a puppy playing with kittens would surely put a smile on her face!

The mother cat, black all over, was sitting on a bare mattress on the bed. When I bounded in, she leaped to her feet with the most astonishing sound I'd ever heard. It was sort of a snarl and sort of a wail. Her ears were flat against her head, and with her fur fluffed out all over, she looked twice my size! Her mouth was open wide, and she hissed, showing all her teeth. They looked very sharp.

From the bed beside the angry mother, there came a sound of frantic, high-pitched mewing. Kittens leaped off the bed and raced in all directions, even faster than Stripes and Blotchy ran when we'd played Chase Me. A gray kitten disappeared under the dresser, two with yellowish stripes dove beneath the bed, and a little black one disappeared, though I could not see where. On the bed, a white kitten backed up her mother by hissing ferociously at me and showing me all her tiny teeth.

"Maggie Rose! Get Lily!" Mom said. "And shut the door so nobody gets out. Quick!"

Chapter 7

I backed away from the two angry cats as Mom walked slowly toward the bed.

"Easy, sweetie, we're here to help," she told the ferocious mother cat.

Maggie Rose shut the door and then bent to grab me. I ran to the opposite side of the bed from Mom and put my front feet upon it, wagging. I was sure that the cats would see that I was a good playmate. My ears were up, my tail was high, and I gave a friendly yip. They'd understand.

The mother did not understand. She retreated, still hissing, and fluffed herself up even bigger. How did she do that? My fur could go up a bit around my neck and shoulders if I wanted to look fierce, but hers could bristle all over her body!

The mother cat was moving away from me, right toward Mom. In one quick movement, Mom got both of her gloved hands around the cat's body. The mother yowled and fought, but Mom held her tightly and sighed with relief. "Okay, I'll get her in a cage and take it downstairs," she told Maggie Rose. "The kittens will be calmer if they can't hear her. See if you can start catching them."

Mom took the struggling mother cat out of the room, closing the door quickly behind her. The white kitten on the bed was still hissing and spitting at me. "Lily, help," Maggie Rose said. She picked me up and dumped me on the bed.

I understood now that this kitten was frightened, just as Missy had been frightened. But I'd shown Missy that I was not scary. I could do the same here.

I crouched down on the bed so I would not tower over the kitten. I squirmed toward her on my belly. The kitten stopped hissing, but she backed away, confused. Maggie Rose swept toward her and scooped her up in her hands.

"There, there, it's okay," she whispered, cuddling the kitten close to her chest and stroking its fur.

That kitten was no longer available to play with, so I jumped down to the floor and poked my nose under the bed. A tiny yellowish paw with tinier claws shot out at me. I jumped back. I jumped forward again. A yellowish face peeked out.

"Good, Lily!" Maggie Rose sang, and she leaned down and swept up the two yellowish kittens. She plopped them on the bed next to the white kitten, who was no longer hissing.

The gray kitten under the dresser was meowing frantically, as if it couldn't get out. Maggie Rose lay down flat on the floor and stuck a hand beneath the piece of furniture. Her hand came out clutching a kitten, which she took to the bed, too.

The white kitten was staring down at me. The two yellowish ones were wandering over the mattress, mewing. Maggie Rose set the gray one down. Then she reached down for me.

"Okay, Lily," she said. "Help them not to be scared."

She put me down on the bed. Kittens scattered and squeaked or sat and stared.

I sat, too, and stared back. These were kittens like Stripes and Blotchy, but I wasn't sure if they wanted to play like Stripes and Blotchy had. Would they puff up and yowl and hiss like the angry mother cat?

No, they wouldn't. They seemed curious about me now that I was sitting down. The white one and one of the yellowish ones came staggering forward on skinny legs to sniff at me.

I stretched out my nose. They sniffed. I sniffed.

Their fear was going away. One of them nuzzled at my cheek. The gray one came toward me, hesitating, ready to run.

I licked his face. He tottered and fell over. One of his sisters pounced on him. They were playing!

I poked my nose between them. Can I play, too?

The little white kitten crouched down. Her rump stuck up. It wiggled. It wasn't exactly like a bow that a dog would make if he or she wanted a game, but it was close. Was she telling me she wanted to play with me?

Yes, she was! She leaped and landed with both front paws around one of mine. She wrestled with my paw and gnawed on it, but her jaws were too weak to really hurt. I picked up my paw and shook it. She tumbled off.

Sitting on the squishy mattress with three paws down and one paw up made me wobble. I fell over.

A yellowish kitten and the gray one came to sniff at my face. The gray one batted at my ear.

Another yellowish one walked over my back. Her tiny claws pricked.

The white kitten sprang at me to seize my paw again and wrestle with it more.

I could tell now that these kittens were even younger than Stripes and Blotchy. That meant I had to be gentle with them. My brothers had never been gentle with me when they wanted to play, but my mother had been. When she wrapped her body around mine or picked me up by the skin on the back of my neck, she'd always been careful not to hurt me.

I could be like that. I could be careful with the kittens.

The door opened. I glanced over and saw Mom standing there. Behind her was the man who smelled like two different dogs.

"Well, would you look at that!" the man said softly.

"Good work, Maggie Rose," Mom praised. She was holding one of those little kennels in her hands. "Okay, let's get them in here while they're all nice and calm."

My girl and Mom started picking up the mewing, squirming kittens and putting them one by one into the little kennel.

The man stood by the door and watched. "Cute little things. What's going to happen to them?" he asked.

"We can always find a home for kittens," Mom said. "Who doesn't love a kitten?"

"Well, my dogs don't," the man said. "But that little pup sure got them to calm right down."

Mom nodded as Maggie Rose picked up a yellowish kitten, the last one left on the bed, and slipped her into the small kennel with her brothers and sisters. "It's because

Lily's still a puppy," she explained. "Young animals are usually seen as nonthreatening, even by other animals. It helps that Lily's so small. The kittens see her as just another baby, like them."

"No," my girl said, fastening the gate on the small kennel as the kittens mewed inside and stuck their little paws through the wires. "It's because Lily's a rescue dog. She just knows what to do."

"Well, maybe," Mom said with a smile as she picked up the kennel full of complaining kittens.

The racket the kittens were making inside the kennel was so loud that I almost missed a panicky meow coming from a different place. There was a closet across the room, with the door propped open just a bit. You'd think that space was too small for any animal to slip inside, but I'd seen the small gray kitten wiggle into a gap beneath the dresser that was not any bigger.

"Come on, time to go," Mom said, and she and Maggie Rose headed for the door.

"Come, Lily!" Maggie Rose called.

I jumped off the bed and hurried to the closet. I put my nose to the crack and could smell kitten inside there.

Small. Female. Frightened and alone.

I pushed at the door with my nose and scratched at it with a paw, but it was stuck. It didn't want to close all the way or open any farther.

"Come on, Lily," my girl urged, coming up behind me. She put her hands underneath my belly and picked me up.

I whined. We should not leave the kitten behind! I knew that wasn't right. The kittens needed to be together, on the bed or in the small kennel. If one of them was all alone, she would feel as lonely and miserable as I'd felt for these last few nights in my kennel.

But Maggie Rose didn't understand. She carried me out of the room and down the staircase. "Stop squirming, Lily!" she said. "Okay, okay, you can get down!"

She set me down on the wooden floor at the foot of the stairs.

The man opened the door for Mom, and she carried the small kennel full of mewing kittens outside.

My girl went out the door, too.

I hesitated. I wanted to follow Maggie Rose. I always wanted to be close to Maggie Rose. But the kitten was all alone upstairs, and I knew that wasn't right.

What should I do?

Maggie Rose would come back for me, I knew. But that kitten wouldn't come out of the closet. Not on her own.

I turned to face the stairs. I hadn't been able to climb them before, but the humans had. It couldn't be *impossible*.

I jumped up to get my front paws on the bottom step.

Then I put as much weight as I could on my front legs and tried to lift my back legs up onto the step as well. It was hard. My claws scrabbled at wood and paint. But at last all four paws were on the first step.

Now I just had to do that again.

Outside, I could hear Mom and my girl talking. "Maggie Rose, can you open the van door for me?" Mom asked. "Let's get these kittens inside. The mother will feel better once she can smell her babies."

"Mom . . . ," said Maggie Rose, hesitating.

The second step now. First front paws. Then back.

"Yes, what?"

I heard the van door opening.

My front paws slipped. I fell back to the first step. *Ouch!*

"Didn't Lily do such a good job? Helping the kittens calm down?"

Mom sighed. "Please, Maggie Rose. Don't start."

I jumped back up and tried again. Front paws jumped. Back paws scrabbled. Pull . . . strain . . . and there! All four paws on step two.

"But, Mom, Lily is . . ." Her voice trailed off. "Where's Lily?"

Chapter 8

My girl's voice called for me. "Lily! Lily, where are you?"

I knew I should go to her . . . and I would. As soon as I finished this job. I was starting to get better at the stairs. Another step, then another, then another. I was climbing!

I heard Maggie Rose's feet coming close to the door. Then I heard the door open. Oh no! She was coming to get me! I had to help the kitty!

I frantically heaved myself up several more steps. My legs were beginning to tire. This was hard work!

"Lily! What are you doing, silly dog?" Maggie Rose started up the stairs after me.

I had to be quick! My legs were starting to tremble, but I still struggled up the last of the stairs, panting. I banged my chin on the floor of the hallway when I shoved my back feet off the final step, but I'd made it! It felt so good to be trotting on a level floor again.

"Lily! Come back!" Maggie Rose was more than half-way up the stairs now. I hurried to the bedroom where we'd found the kittens and their mother.

The door was still open. I ran straight up to the closet and stuck my nose into the gap between the door and the frame. The kitten was still in there. Still alone.

Still scared.

I barked. That made the kitten even more scared, so it was not the right thing to do.

"Maggie Rose!" Mom called from downstairs. "Get Lily and come on!"

"I'm getting her, Mom!" Maggie Rose called back. Her feet were coming down the hallway now.

I pawed at the closet door. It didn't budge. Then I pushed my nose into the crack once more and shoved as hard as I could. I was in!

"Lily!" Maggie Rose was at the bedroom door. "Lily, I saw you. Come out of there!" I heard my girl walking across the bedroom floor.

"Maggie Rose, where are you? What's going on?" Mom was climbing the stairs now.

Along the back wall of the closet was a stack of cardboard boxes. The kitten was behind them, just like Freddie had been behind the cages when we'd been playing Chase Me. But Freddie had been happy. This kitten was not happy. I could smell fear and misery.

I pushed my nose into the gap between a box and the wall. There was the kitten, huddled in a quivering ball of black fur. I nudged her with my nose. She only curled up tighter.

This was a very tiny kitten. I was bigger than she was, just as my mother was bigger than I was.

This kitten needed to leave this space. It could not stay here all alone.

"Lily, what are you doing? We have to go! Come on!" Grunting, Maggie Rose yanked the closet door all the way open.

I knew what to do with a tiny creature that needed to be somewhere else. Very gently, just as my mother used to do with me, I picked the kitten up by the loose skin at the back of her neck. She did not struggle. She hung limply from my mouth as I backed away from the boxes, toward my girl.

Maggie Rose gasped.

She retreated into the bedroom, giving me room to turn around. I did it carefully. I did not want to startle the kitten or hurt her neck.

"Mom, look," Maggie Rose said softly. "Look what Lily did!"

I heard Mom draw in her breath.

"Another kitten," she whispered. "In the closet? Oh, Maggie Rose. Oh, Lily. We almost left her here!"

"Mom, she would have starved!"

"I know, honey." Mom nodded. "I know."

I carried the kitten to my girl's feet and gently put her down. The kitten sat, looking around in a daze. Maggie Rose bent down and picked her up as tenderly as possible.

"Lily, good girl," she whispered as the scared kitten cuddled against her chest.

"Yes. Lily, you are a good, good dog," Mom said. She knelt down and stroked me. "Such a good dog."

Maggie Rose gave the black kitten to Mom and picked me up to carry me back downstairs. I was relieved that I did not have to climb *down* the stairs. Stairs were hard work!

"Let's get the cats back to the shelter," Mom said as we walked outside.

She put the black kitten into the kennel with her litter-mates, and Maggie Rose slid into the back seat with me. I

was tired from all the excitement of playing with the kittens and climbing the stairs. I settled down for a nice doze on Maggie Rose's lap.

"Mom . . . ," Maggie Rose said as the van started to move.

"Honey, I know what you're about to say," Mom said.

"But can't you see what Lily did? She rescued that kitten! Mom, she saved it!"

"I know, Maggie Rose. I know."

"She was born to be a rescue dog!"

I could feel Maggie Rose's anger and fear and sadness trembling through her. Why was she so upset? No kittens were in trouble anymore.

I sat up to stretch my head toward Maggie Rose's face. Her neck was as high as I could reach. I licked her under her chin. I just didn't know what else to do to make her happy.

Maggie Rose didn't say anything more. Mom didn't say anything. The van drove.

Then the van stopped while a light shone up ahead. Mom turned to look around at Maggie Rose and me, and she smiled.

"You're right," she said. "Lily *is* a rescue dog."

Maggie Rose gasped. I gazed at her curiously.

Mom nodded. "We'll find a different puppy for the DJ. Lily can stay with us."

If you enjoyed *Lily to the Rescue*, you'll love these Puppy Tales by W. Bruce Cameron:

EVERY DOG HAS A PURPOSE. ELLIE'S IS THE MOST IMPORTANT OF ALL.

ellie's story

A DOG'S PURPOSE PUPPY TALE

W. Bruce Cameron

AN IRRESISTIBLE TALE OF A DOG AND HIS BOY

BAILEY'S STORY

A DOG'S PURPOSE PUPPY TALE

W. Bruce Cameron

A HEARTWARMING TALE OF A DOG AND HER GIRL

MOLLY'S STORY

A DOG'S PURPOSE PUPPY TALE

W. Bruce Cameron

LITTLE DOG IN THE BIG CITY

max's story

A DOG'S PURPOSE PUPPY TALE

W. Bruce Cameron

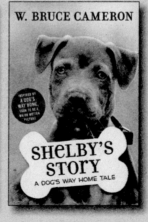

W. BRUCE CAMERON

INSPIRED BY A DOG'S WAY HOME, SOON TO BE A MAJOR MOTION PICTURE

SHELBY'S STORY

A DOG'S WAY HOME TALE

About the Author

W. Bruce Cameron is the *New York Times* bestselling author of *A Dog's Purpose*, *A Dog's Journey*, *A Dog's Way Home*, and the young-reader novels *Ellie's Story*, *Bailey's Story*, *Molly's Story*, *Max's Story*, *Shelby's Story*, and *Toby's Story*. He lives with his wife, Cathryn, and his dog, Tucker, in California.